Lauren and

Lucky

Kelly McKain

THIS DIARY BELONGS TO

Lauren

Dear Riders,

A warm welcome to Sunnyside Stables!

Sunnyside is our home and for the next week it will be yours, too! My husband Johnny and I have two children, Millie and James, plus two dogs ... and all the ponies, of course!

We have friendly yard staff and a very talented instructor, Sally, to help you get the most out of your week. If you have any worries or questions about anything at all, just ask. We're here to help, and we want your holiday to be as enjoyable as possible – so don't be shy!

As you know, you will have a pony to look after as your own for the week. Your pony can't wait to meet you and start having fun! During your stay, you'll be caring for your pony, improving your riding, learning new skills and making new friends. And this week we're off to the Dorset County Show, where you'll see some fabulous dressage and lots of exciting stalls and displays. Add swimming, games and films, and you're in for a fun-filled holiday to remember!

This special Pony Camp Diary is for you to fill with your holiday memories. We hope you'll write all about your adventures here at Sunnyside Stables – because we know you're going to have lots!

Wishing you a wonderful time with us!

Jody xx

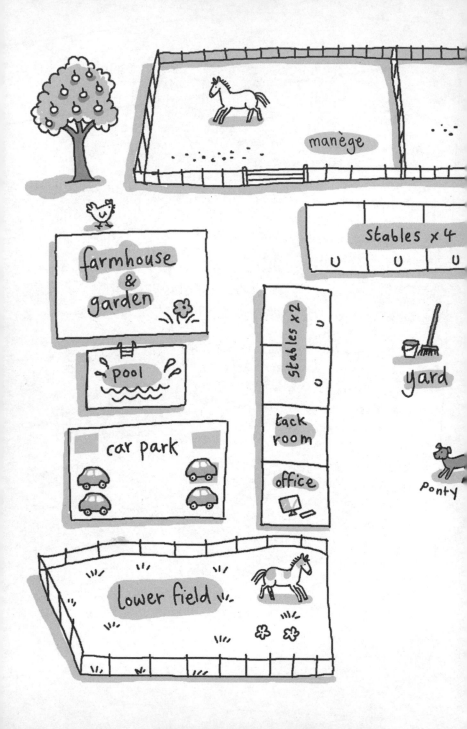

Monday lunchtime –
here I am at Pony Camp!

Us girls are sitting on the benches outside the farmhouse in the sunshine, and we've all decided to start our diaries at the same time! It's been fantastic here so far – I've met all these fab girls, been given a brilliant pony and we've had our first riding lesson. Wow! I've just realized that I've got loads to say so I'll try writing really quickly!

By the time me and Mum got here most of the other girls had already arrived and unpacked their stuff. Mum had to rush straight off again 'cos she'd left my three smelly brothers in the car, so Jody (who runs Pony Camp) showed me up to my room. All the way up the stairs I was babbling on about how I'd specially chosen to come this week because there's a chance to

do dressage. I've done a few tests at shows
near where I live on Fizz or Gregory, the ponies
I ride at my local stables, and I'm really excited
about learning more. And it's great 'cos some
of the girls here are as dressage mad as me!
My horsy friends back home are crazy on
showjumping instead, so I don't normally get
to talk about dressage that much.

When me and Jody got up to the room, the
top bunk was already bagsied by a girl called
Arabella, so I took the bottom one. The messy
bed by the window turned out to be Jody's
daughter Millie's. She's really nice – in fact,
everyone here is.

After we'd said our names, Arabella was like,
"Well, the girls in the oldest room all came

together and Millie'll be riding

*YOU'LL
HAVE TO BY MY
FRIEND!*

in the other group 'cos she's

not into dressage, so *you'll*

have to be my friend." I couldn't

work out if she was joking or not, but she just

smiled and put her arm
through mine and we
went down to the yard
together. That's where
we met the other girls,
and we were all saying
hi and telling each
other what riding
we've done and
that kind of thing.

   After Sally showed us round the yard and
gave us a safety talk it was time to meet our
ponies. We all stood in the yard feeling really
excited as Lydia the stable girl brought them
out one by one and helped us mount up. Sally
said usually we would have an assessment
lesson to work out which groups we'll be in,
but this week we don't need one 'cos there'll
just be a dressage group and a normal group.

The dressage group (Group B) is:

Paula, age 12, who's Spanish, with **Flame**.

Leonie, also 12, who's half German and is Paula's best friend, with **Charm**.

Marie, Leonie's younger sister, who's 10 like me, with **Mischief**.

Arabella, also 10, with **Gracie**, her own pony (who's a sweet Arab mare with a cute snip on her nose) – how lucky is that!

Me, **Lauren**, and (drum roll please!) the most gorgeous, cute pony I have ever seen, my lovely **LUCKY!**

I couldn't believe my luck when Sally said he was for me. My LUCK in getting LUCKY – hee hee! He's beautiful – a 10-year-old 14hh blue roan cob with this cascading flowing mane, cute clumpy feet and *the* most beautiful eyes.

Arabella said, "Oh dear, Lauren, don't you think he's a bit clumpy for dressage?" But I just pointed out how well Charlotte Dujardin does on Valegro, who's a heavier build, and Stephanie Croxford with Mr President, who the crowd absolutely LOVE. Arabella looked a bit surprised and muttered, "Fair point."

I gave Lucky an extra pat just in case he knew she was not being that nice about him.

As I said, Millie's riding with Group A, 'cos she reckons her pony Tally doesn't exactly get the concept of dressage and is only really happy when he's dragging her through a hedge!

The others in Group A are:

Polly, who is 8, riding **Jewel**.

Bea, who's 8, on crazy **Cracker**.

And **Jojo**, only just 7, on **Sugar**.

Sally

Jody

Sally taught our group, and Jody taught Group A. We were nervous and excited as we mounted up and made our way to the manège. But we didn't suddenly start doing really hard dressage movements or anything – it was just a normal lesson for Sally to see what we can do.

It was brilliant riding Lucky. He's really chilled out, which is great, but he's not exactly quick off the leg! I'll have to get him to perk up for the dressage test, somehow.

While we were walking round on a long rein to warm down, Sally told us she's got a surprise in store, but she's not going to reveal it until this afternoon. Of course, we were all begging her to tell us straight away, but she just did a zipping her lips sign and looked mysterious.

When the lesson finished we all dismounted and ran up our stirrups, and Sally asked Leonie to lead the way back to the barn to untack. Then when we reached the yard, Arabella tried to hand Gracie's reins to Lydia.

Lydia laughed and said, "Nice try, but we all look after our own ponies here, that's the point!"

Arabella laughed too and said, "'Course. Only joking!" But I didn't really know if she was or not. How strange! I'd be desperate to do everything I could for my pony if I had one. Especially if it was my gorgeous Lucky! I'd do anything for *him*!

Lucky was so funny in the barn. Like, when I was grooming him he kept turning his head and trying to eat the body brush. He also nudged the tack box over with his nose, to see if there were any Polos at the bottom, probably! I love him so much already, and when I gave him a big pat and stroke he did a happy snort and nuzzled into my shoulder, so I think he loves me, too.

Lucky *Loves* Lauren

Arabella was waiting by the barn door for me so we could go in for lunch together, but I had to keep popping back to see Lucky! She just stood there, going, "Hurry up, I'm hungry!" so I gave him a last hug and then I gave Gracie one too, so she didn't feel left out.

For lunch we had chicken and salad and—

Oh, we're all off to the yard now. Sally's going to reveal her surprise! Well, fast writing worked, 'cos I got down nearly everything we've done so far!

What a brilliant surprise!

We're about to have our workshop and I'm just quickly scribbling this while Sally's gone to find the pens for the whiteboard. The surprise is:

 We're going to create our own dressage tests, set to MUSIC!

I know from watching the Winter Dressage Championships on *Horse and Country TV* that this is called freestyle. It's my fave type of dressage and it's so cool to see the horses moving in time to the music. We even get to pick what movements we want to do and choose our own tunes, too! It'll be just like doing dance routines, but on our ponies!

Well, *obviously* everyone was really excited about it and instantly started chatting about what music they might pick. Arabella did get a bit worried that we won't be doing "proper" dressage tests like the official ones at comps, but Sally promised her that we'll be taking the technical side very seriously and the movements will have to be absolutely spot on. Plus, there are going to be some things in it we *all* have to do (called the compulsory movements) so she can compare us more easily. We were all a bit nervous, but Sally said not to worry as we'll build up our routines step by step. Phew!

Marie had the idea of doing the comp in fancy dress then, and started saying how she wanted to do Mischief up as a pop star and dye his mane with different colour hair mascaras and put purple legwarmers on him!

We all laughed when Sally said, "I don't think Mischief would be too happy about that, seeing as he's a boy!"

But she did agree that some kind of themed dress to go with our music might be fun.

Arabella said she's just bought a brand-new regulation dressage competition jacket and jodhs and she's wearing *them*, so there! Sally smiled and said that's fine, too.

Even more exciting, when we have our trip out to the Dorset County Show on Wednesday, Sally says we'll be seeing some freestyle dressage to music in one of the show rings. So we'll be able to get some tips from the pros, as well!

Oh, she's back, gotta go…

After tea

We're all going swimming soon, but Jody says we have to let our tea go down for half an hour first. Hopefully that's enough time to write about what happened this afternoon!

When Sally came back, we started off talking about the most important elements of dressage, and she wrote a list of things like rhythm and balance and expression, and also that "the aim is to get yourself and your pony moving as one, in harmony".

I reckon me and Lucky can manage that – we're such a good team already!

Then Sally explained the compulsory movements. She said we could work them into our own routines however we wanted, but that it's a good idea to make everything flowing and symmetrical (i.e. to do each thing twice, once on each rein). She said this is also a good idea because if you don't get something right on one rein you still have another chance to show the judges you can do it – clever, huh?

Here's the list of compulsory movements:

Medium walk

Working trot (and also show a few lengthened strides)

20 metre circle

Working canter

Rein back 4 steps (tricky!) →

We can also add other stuff like 10m circles, turns, all the other transitions (well, maybe not halt to canter, or even walk to canter, not for me anyway!), serpentines and free walk on a long rein. Leonie wants to do counter-canter in hers, which is mega-difficult! Sally says it's a possibility and we'll see how we get on. With so much choice of what to do, our routines are going to be really different from each other!

WOW !

When it was time for our lesson we were already massively excited and we'd all started having ideas about what we might put in our routines. We were still chatting away as we warmed up in the manège and Sally had to tell us to calm down and concentrate! As we were walking and trotting round on each rein, she explained that one of the cornerstones of dressage is getting good impulsion, which means, well, not *speed* exactly, but more like power through the pony's hindquarters. I don't know exactly how to explain it, but I do know that Lucky and I didn't have much of it! He did wake up a bit when we did loads of turns, circles, half halts and transitions, though. Sally said he's much more expressive in his movements when I get him going just that extra bit more, so if I can improve his impulsion I should have expression sorted out, too.

Flame has no problem being expressive, she's as much of a drama queen as Paula and they look great together!

Drama Queens

Their work was brilliant from the start — and even during the warm-up they were sailing round in this beautiful springy trot like complete pros. Marie's working trot looked nice and even, too — once she'd got Mischief actually *on* the track, that is! And Leonie seems to be able to get Charm to halt exactly at the marker, never leaving a leg behind. I wish me and Lucky could do that!

When we practised the compulsory movements one by one I found the working trot quite tricky, and Lucky didn't at all get what I was asking for in the rein back.

But, can you believe it, Arabella said she thought it was all easy-peasy! Sally smiled and said, "Well, of course you can easily do each thing on its *own*, but it's putting the movements together and hitting specific markers that's far more challenging."

Unlike Charm, Lucky doesn't seem that interested in making transitions exactly at the right markers, and that's something I really need to work on – well, something *else*! I don't mind, though, there's plenty of time to improve on everything. And I love how relaxed Lucky is; it's part of his character and I wouldn't want him to be any different!

I kind of wish Arabella would chill out a bit, though. I don't think she *was* joking when she said I'd *have* to be her friend. She sticks to me like glue, and doesn't have much to say to the other girls.

I don't mind, well, not *really* really, but it is a bit annoying when I'm chatting to Marie or Millie and she just comes up and drags me off. Also, she can be a bit mean about people. Like, when we were untacking she was going, "Can you believe Marie suggested hair mascaras and legwarmers for Mischief! How ridiculous!"

I felt really awkward 'cos she wasn't exactly saying it very quietly and I thought Marie might hear (she was only in the next pen with Leonie and their ponies). I hate it when girls gossip about each other – I just don't see the point.

So I said, "She was only being keen." Arabella got cross with me then out of nowhere and went, "Huh! Whose side are you *on?*" So I got annoyed back and said, "I don't think there are *sides.*"

HUH!

She just gave me a huffy look and began putting everything back in her tack box. That's when I realized she hadn't picked out Gracie's feet. I didn't feel like saying anything, seeing as she was being so moody with me, but on the other hand I didn't want Gracie to have a bit of wood chipping or a stone stuck in her foot for the rest of the day. When I mentioned it, Arabella went, "I was going to do it now, *actually,*" in this really stroppy way. I don't know why she was so prickly about it. We all forget things now and again. It's no big deal.

Oh well, never mind. I've got other things to think about – like the dressage! At tea Leonie and Paula were talking about *lateral flexion* and I was like, oh help!

When I said how me and Lucky will be lucky even to get round, never mind anything fancy, they were really sweet and started going, "Oh, I know how you feel, I'm so rubbish," and "Don't worry, I'll never make it through a whole routine," even though they are BRILLIANT. How nice is that?! My brothers would just say, "Yeah, you suck, loser!"

I wanted to sit and talk to them for longer, but Arabella dragged me off to look at her make-up collection.

Oh, gotta go – it's time to head over to the pool!

Tuesday after lunch –
I'm just writing in here while Leonie and Paula are clearing up ('cos it's their turn on the rota)

Swimming was fun last night – we all played water games and had comps together as a big group. Me and Arabella had such a cool time after lights out, too. Just as I was falling asleep, she shook my arm and suggested a midnight feast. I wanted to wake Millie as well, but Arabella said she only had two of the Sherbert Dib Dabs and it might be awkward 'cos it's not the kind of thing you can share out. So I climbed up on to her bunk and we scoffed her secret stash of sweets and chatted, but in whispers so that Jody didn't hear us.

She was telling me about the amazing posh boarding school she goes to – she keeps Gracie in the stables there and she can ride her every single day. Imagine living at a boarding school with your pony! And think of the midnight feasts and the fun you'd have with the other girls. It must be like being at Pony Camp *all the time*! Honestly, her life sounds fabulous! *And* she's going on loads of different holiday schemes, doing everything from drama to learning French actually in France. *And* she says her parents let her do whatever she wants, 'cos they live in Hong Kong and she only has to see them, like, twice a year or something.

So anyway, when she said all that, there I was, staring with my mouth open. "Wow, you are so, so, *so* lucky, you are lucky times one million!" I said.

Lucky...Lucky...Lucky...×1million

30

"*My* dad's really strict and
my school friends live
miles away so I'm stuck
with my three yucky
brothers most of the
time. And somehow
they always seem to

wriggle out of their chores, but Mum never
lets *me* off. If it wasn't for my riding lesson on
Saturday mornings, I'd go mad! I wish I could
be you and always have girls to hang around
with, and my own pony to ride and spend
time with whenever I wanted to – it sounds
like heaven to me!"

When I said all this to Arabella, she just
shrugged and said, "Yeah, I guess so." She
didn't seem that enthusiastic, but I know she
was only playing it down so as not to rub it in.
We fell asleep soon after that, so we didn't talk
about it any more.

Normally I hate getting up in the mornings, but it was brilliant this morning 'cos it was the first day of waking up at Pony Camp.

After breakfast we grabbed some lead ropes from the tack room and went straight off up the lane to the upper field to catch our ponies. I went up to Lucky and gave him a pat and a carrot and he let me catch him straight away. I also helped Bea get her lead rope on Cracker because the clip was quite stiff and he kept moving his head about, the cheeky boy! Gracie was being a bit flighty and kept running away from Arabella, so she asked Lydia to catch her instead.

It was so nice all clip-clopping back down the lane with our ponies and grooming them in the barn together, all chatting and joking – just how I'd imagined Pony Camp would be!

For our dressage workshop, our group sat at the picnic benches outside the barn. The second

Sally appeared, we started bombarding her with ideas for our routines, and asking questions about the compulsory movements.

"Hang on! Hang on!" she cried. "I'm glad you're keen, but one at a time!"

So we shot our hands up like we were at school, and got into fits of giggles about that. Once she'd answered our questions, Sally explained that most people find it  easiest to make up the routine first and then choose music to go with it. You can have two or three different tunes put together or stick to just one, if it fits well. She gave us some really good advice, which is to think about our ponies' personalities and choose the movements that suit their strengths rather than the ones that highlight their weaknesses (so me and Lucky won't be doing any halt to canter transitions then!).

Then Sally sent Leonie
to the games room to
get some rulers and
pencils and paper, and
we all copied her scale
drawing of the arena
off the whiteboard,
like this ─────────→

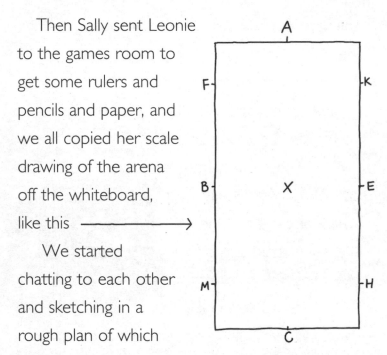

We started
chatting to each other
and sketching in a
rough plan of which
set movements we could do and the best order
to do them in. There was lots of rubbing out
too, when we realized that you can't link certain
ones up very easily! There weren't enough
rubbers to go round, so Arabella broke hers in
half and shared with me. We had this good idea
of doing a twenty metre circle in trot in the AX
half of the school so that when we've done the

circle we can go into canter in the AF corner
and it should look really cool. Sally came and
leaned over us and said she liked that idea, and
we felt really pleased with ourselves!

In our lesson this morning we worked
without stirrups so we could improve our
balance for the dressage. Mischief
did a big plunge when he went
into canter and Marie almost
went out the side door, but
she managed to grab the
pommel in time!

We worked on the set movements again
and I think me and Lucky are actually improving.
We had a go at the 20 metre circle in trot and
then at getting canter in the AF corner, the
sequence Arabella and I had thought up. It
worked really well, so we're definitely putting it
in our routines! We also tried out trotting down
the centre line, then doing medium walk from

C to E, then going back into trot at E. Sally's right, it is tricky when you start putting things together and trying to hit the markers.

I also remembered what she'd said about Lucky needing preparation so I sat up tall and gave him a few extra squeezes with my legs to get his walk more active before I asked for trot. It worked on the third try (and yes, bang on the marker!). I'm *so* putting that combination in my test.

Oh, time to get back on to the yard. Bye!

After tea – well, it's not my fault if Arabella wants to be a moody pants!

Arabella

MOODY

I just can't work out why she was so mean to me in the lesson, and in front of everyone else, too! She was fine at lunch, so perhaps she got in a mood because of what happened in this afternoon's dressage workshop. But I don't get *why* – it was nothing really.

We were at the picnic benches again, sketching out rough ideas for our dressage tests with Sally going round helping us. Me and Marie were pacing ours out in front of the barn, as if we were on our ponies, and we got in hysterical giggles 'cos I was whinnying like Lucky does, and Marie was demonstrating round-the-worlds with no pony, which mainly involved twirling while kicking her legs in the air. Then she even asked

Sally if we could do them in the comp! Sally said
she thought we were crazy girls, but we could if
we wanted to. Arabella said we couldn't because
it's not an official dressage move, but Sally said,
"Well, it's my competition and my rules, so if it
makes things even more fun, then why not?"

So maybe Arabella was
moody 'cos she didn't
get her own way? But
still, I don't get why she
should care what
someone *else* is doing.

Anyway, I know she was *definitely* in a huff
when we went to get ready for our lesson. We
had a bit of extra time because Sally was busy
in the manège working one to one with Emily,
the local girl who rides Emerald, Sunnyside's
new pony. So Lydia supervised us on the yard
and Marie tried to help me work out how
to smarten Lucky up a bit for the final comp.

We started a mane
plait, and can you
believe, Arabella
said, "I don't know
why you're bothering,
he's so cobby he's
not going to look smart whatever you do!"

I mean, char-ming! I went bright red and
hugged Lucky's neck. "Yes, he will. He'll look
fab. Won't you, sweetie?" I said loudly, but
Arabella had already wandered away.

When Marie went to help Jojo pick out
Sugar's hooves, Arabella came stomping back
and said I was *going off* with her! I said, "Marie
was helping me, what's wrong with that?" but
Arabella got all moody and wouldn't lend me
her dandy brush to get the woodchip dust out
of Lucky's hind fetlock feather. I don't
understand why she acts like she owns me!
We're all here to enjoy our ponies and learn

dressage and have a good time, so what's the
point of making problems when there aren't any?

And then in the lesson the WORST thing
happened.

Once we'd warmed up in the manège, Sally
said we were going to practise the combination
of dressage movements again, but this time in
pairs. She explained that this was a good
exercise because the more forward-going,
confident ponies would give the others a boost.
She said Arabella would lead me and Leonie
would lead Marie and she was just about to
explain what Paula was going to do when
Arabella said, "We're not doing the *actual*
competition in pairs, are we? Because it's not
fair for *them* to affect my score." When she said
them she looked at me and Lucky like we were
a couple of complete no-hopers.

I was shocked and I
automatically reached down
and stroked Lucky's neck. I
felt really embarrassed that
she'd said that in front of
everyone and also really
angry that she could be so

mean about us. Sally was cross too. "It's only for
this lesson," she snapped at Arabella, who just
looked sulkily back at her.

"*I'd* like to go with Lauren. I think she's
brilliant," said Paula, coming to my rescue.

Sally said, "Yes, all right then, lovely. And
Leonie, you can take Arabella over after you've
worked with Marie."

Arabella gave me a mean look as if it was

MY fault that she wasn't one
of the leaders any more,
when it was HER who'd
made a fuss. I know

she's a bit of a perfectionist about the dressage, but that's no reason to be so horrible!

The rest of the lesson went OK, but it was hard to forget about what Arabella had said and I couldn't concentrate as much as usual. Maybe poor Lucky was upset, too, because he didn't seem himself either. Between us we were even sloppier about making transitions exactly at the markers and we didn't get our canter in the AF corner either, so I had to ride another 20 metre circle in trot and ask again.

But we did finally cheer up a bit when we got to the pairs work, 'cos Lucky really went blazing round after Flame and Paula. I think Flame's showmanship must have inspired him, because he did everything with a lot of style – Sally was right, it *is* easier with someone to copy. She said how good we were, and how much we'd come on already and I couldn't help grinning. It really boosted my confidence after what Arabella said.

I don't care what she thinks – I'm so proud of my lovely boy!

In the second half of the lesson, we all went out of the gate and stood by the fence. Then one by one we went back into the manège and tried out our routines. Lydia came and sat on the spectators' stand and called out our sequences for us. It was all very rough and messy, and we kept stopping when things didn't work and changing them, with Sally's help, and Lydia wrote the new things down on our papers.

Lucky tried hard, but he got a bit confused because some of the things I'd put down were quite awkward for him. So my routine changed a lot in the end as Sally and I found ways to make it smoother. When Lydia gave me my

paper back it was very scribbly, so I redrew
it up neatly, like this:

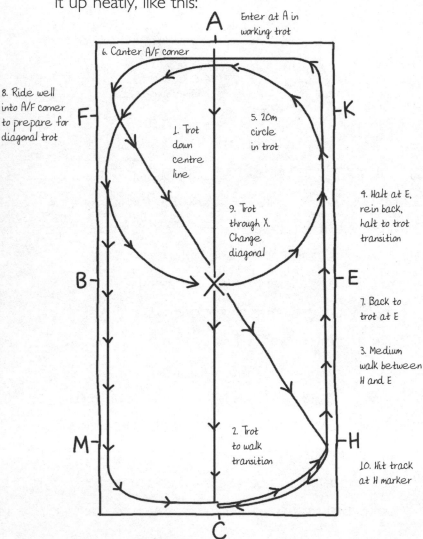

A — Enter at A in working trot

6. Canter A/F corner

8. Ride well into A/F corner to prepare for diagonal trot

F

K

1. Trot down centre line

5. 20m circle in trot

9. Trot through X. Change diagonal

B

E

4. Halt at E, rein back, halt to trot transition

7. Back to trot at E

3. Medium walk between H and E

M

2. Trot to walk transition

H

10. Hit track at H marker

C

11. At C trot down centre line, then at A turn right and repeat sequence on other rein

Oh, I just have to also write that Leonie's routine was amazing! She's got these serpentines in it that look really beautiful and she even had a go at counter-canter. Because she did it so well, Sally said she could leave it in.

At the end of the lesson Sally said well done to all of us and also that now is the time to start sorting out our music. Jody's going to help us with that tonight – so hopefully I'll get inspired when I hear a few different things!

On the yard Arabella kept trying to chat to me, but 'cos I didn't really feel like talking to her she started going, "What's wrong?" And I kept saying "Nothing" because I couldn't be bothered to go into it – I just wanted to focus on Lucky.

Then she said, "Oh Lauren, it's not that little thing I said in the lesson, is it?"

I got really cross then because it wasn't a little thing, it was a great big GIANT thing. I stopped sweeping and leaned on my broom and said, "You say you're my friend, but you're so mean to me ... and to Lucky."

Arabella rolled her eyes. "'Course I'm your friend, silly!" she insisted. "You can't get cross just because I want the best possible chance to win the competition. As we're friends, you should *want* me to do well. Don't be so sensitive!"

I WAS ABSOLUTELY FUMING then and it took me a few seconds to be able to speak. By the time I did, she'd flounced off somewhere else. When she didn't come back I filled up Gracie's water bucket and finished off combing her mane. It wasn't fair for her to suffer just 'cos Arabella was having a sulk! It's so strange how she doesn't seem bothered about looking after Gracie. She's such a sweet and gorgeous pony – if she was mine I'd want to spend every single second I could with her!

So it isn't surprising that I didn't sit with Arabella at tea! Instead I went out to the picnic tables, and luckily Leonie called me over to sit with her and Paula and Marie. We had fun talking through our freestyle routines and I did my best not to look at Arabella, who was sitting with the younger ones on the next table. When she walked past us to get seconds from the buffet in the kitchen she did this deliberate looking the other way thing. Leonie did this sort of "ooooh" raised eyebrows thing at me and I did it back.

Oh, I wish Arabella would lighten up! I've been dreaming about my holiday at Pony Camp for months, ever since Mum said I could go, and in my imagination there certainly wasn't a moody girl making things difficult for me. This is my chance to be one of the girls and I want us all to be a big, happy group hanging out together – I'm not going to let Arabella spoil everything!

I'm writing this in bed, after my shower and hot chocolate, waiting for Jody to come and turn the lights out

Last night at this time we were all chatting away, but tonight Millie's already fast asleep and Arabella's reading a magazine. She's turning the pages really loudly to show how much she's ignoring me. Oh well, I don't care — I wanted time to write in here anyway.

I still haven't had any inspiration about my music. Leonie played me a few songs on her iPod, but none of them were quite right. I also had a look through Millie's CDs, but nothing stood out. It was really funny helping the others choose, though. We had songs playing through the computer in the games room and when Paula and Marie picked theirs (which are these two pieces of flamenco music for Paula and this song about being in trouble for Marie) we were working out which bits went with which movements.

The younger ones wanted to join in too, so me, Leonie and Marie gave Polly, Bea and Jojo piggybacks around the room, pretending to be the ponies while marking out the dressage steps that Paula was calling out.

Arabella was a bit on her own, but then Millie started asking her about her routine and stuff, and helping her choose some music from Jody's Popular Classics CD set, so she wasn't completely left out. Anyway, it's not up to me to worry about her – not after how she's been!

Then Jody said we could just about squeeze
in a swim if we were quick and we all decided
to carry on playing ponies in the pool. I gave
Jojo a piggyback this time (much easier in the
water!). We pretended the pool was the
manège and Leonie played the part of Sally and
stood in the middle giving us instructions.

Arabella gave Millie a piggyback for a while,
but then she decided she wanted to do some
serious swimming to get fit for the dressage
comp, so Leonie took Millie round instead.
Then we persuaded *Jody* to be Sally and do the
calling out, even though she thought we were
all completely mad!

I feel so much better now I've spent more
time with the other girls. It's a shame that
Arabella was a bit left out, but it was her choice.

Oh, Jody's coming up the stairs! Time for
lights out. Goodnight!

Wednesday — back at Sunnyside. We had an amazing day at the Dorset County Show!

There were no yard duties this morning as we had to head straight off in the minibus, but we did take some carrots up to the pony field first, so I got to see my gorgeous Lucky before we left.

I sat next to Marie on the way. She let me listen to one headphone of her iPod, but I didn't get any inspiration for my dressage music from it (I did have an idea later, though!). It took us about an hour to get to the show, and Arabella just sat on her own with her mags spread out on the seat next to her and she didn't talk to anyone the entire way. But when we got there she was going, "Wow!" like everyone else because the show was far bigger that we'd imagined, with tons and tons of people everywhere, and loads of cute dogs.

When we first got there we had a wander round the stalls. There was this one with gorgeous silver jewellery on it, and we all tried on different rings and necklaces and stuff, until Jody had to drag us away!

Then Sally called us over to the Barn Owl Trust stand, where we got to see Barney. He was gorgeous and really soft, and we had to be very quiet because he was also quite shy. Then we looked at the Handmade Soap Co. stand where they had all these lovely wedges of soaps. They looked like sweets and smelt delicious – like, there were berry ones, and peppermint ones and even chocolate and toffee.

I used some of my spending money to buy one
for Nana and one for Mum. Smelling the toffee
soap made us want some real toffee so Jody
took us over to the Dorset Fudge Company
stand and we all bought something to munch
on as we went round (I got vanilla flavour).

When the dressage comp started, loads of
people came over to watch. Sally explained that
dressage to music is really popular, even with
people who aren't into horses.

The competition was fantastic – the riders
were so smart and the horses were beautifully
turned out. They did amazingly tricky
movements like piaffe and passage and even
some one-time changes, which are so cool 'cos
it looks like the horse is skipping. We all had
our faves who we wanted to win – mine was
this lady called Felicity Harper on this gorgeous
bay, Chakaboom. I liked them because she was
a fab rider and Chakaboom was quite cobby,

like Lucky. They did really well and
the crowd all loved them
(*so there*, Arabella!). And
guess what, they came
second – not quite top, but
pretty fab!

Afterwards, Jody had arranged for us to go
into the horsebox area and meet some of the
competitors. I was really nervous and I didn't
think I'd know what to say, but then I spotted
Felicity sitting on the steps of Chakaboom's
trailer, cleaning his tack. I was so keen to tell her
how fab I thought she was that I completely
forgot about feeling shy and just walked over
there. I got her autograph, which I'm sticking in
here for safekeeping:

> *Good luck in your dressage comp,*
> *Lauren and Lucky!*
>
> *Love, Felicity Harper*

Before I knew it, I was telling her about how I really want me and Lucky to do well on Friday, but how I don't think we will, not with him being so laid-back.

She said, "Chak can be a bit like that, too, but just be positive and confident and I'm sure you'll inspire Lucky to do his very best. If you play to his strengths, you'll be fine."

So that got me thinking, and then in the minibus on the way back I got struck with inspiration! We were all having a singalong of songs from our fave musicals and after we'd done that "oh oh ooooh!" song from *Grease*, Leonie started us all off singing "I'd Do Anything" from *Oliver*. I suddenly realized *that* would be the perfect dressage song for me and Lucky, because we really *would* do anything for

each other! Lucky is such
a scruffy urchin he'll
make the perfect Oliver
(and it fits his character
because he's honest, loyal
and doesn't give up). I'm
going to be Nancy and I might
even come into the arena twirling an old
umbrella, which also shows off the fact that
Lucky isn't easily spooked!

Scruffy Urchin →

When we got back I told Sally my idea and
she thought it was fab! I'm so excited that I've
found the perfect song! Jody downloaded it on
to the computer for me and we had a listen
while I helped her set out
some squash and biscuits
(we were thirsty after all that singing!).

Oh, guess what? Sally's just come in and
said we can go and see our ponies up in the
field – bye!

Wednesday at 9.42p.m. – I'm writing this in bed by the light of my torch

The others have gone to sleep. I did try, but I couldn't stop thinking about everything that happened this evening. I'm writing it all down in here because hopefully then my brain will be able to switch off!

After we'd all had showers, we got into our pyjamas and I went into the older girls' room so us four could practise our dressage tests and help each other learn our sequences off by heart. It was really funny, 'cos we were doing it like a quiz show and when we got something wrong, Paula was going, "Beep! Incorrect answer. Goodbye!"

Arabella came and joined in with us when she'd had her shower. Everything was fine at first, but when I was in the hot seat I said my trot down the centre line the wrong way round, CXA instead of AXC. Paula did the beep, but then Arabella chipped in, shouting, "Incorrect answer! You are rubbish! Please leave the competition! In fact, don't even bother entering! You've got no chance of winning on that lazy, scruffy pony anyway!"

I was almost shaking – I just couldn't believe she'd been *that* horrible to me!

Everyone else was staring at her, but she just burst into fits of giggles – she obviously thought she was being *funny*!

Then Leonie said to her, "Why don't you buzz off!" and Paula added, "We

didn't even invite you. You came barging in and now you're ruining things." Even Marie mumbled, "Yeah," really quietly.

Arabella looked surprised at first, and then her eyes filled up with tears and she ran out of the room.

After that the others had a moan about her and I didn't join in at first, but then I thought, *Well, why not, after she's been so mean to me?* So I told them what she'd said about Marie wanting to make Mischief look like a pop star, and about how I've been looking after Gracie, as well as Lucky, when she's been too lazy to bother.

Then when we were downstairs having our hot chocolate, the phone rang and Jody said it was my mum. I stood round the corner in the porch bit talking to her, 'cos it was too loud in the kitchen, and I told her all about everything I've been up to here at Pony Camp. I even had a quick chat with each of my brothers – I was amazed they wanted to speak to me, they're normally too busy playing outside! Then Mum came back on to say goodbye, and when I put the phone down I turned round and there was Arabella, listening in! She went, "I love you, Mum!" – copying me, but in a mean way.

I was like, "So what? It's my *mum*!"

Arabella pulled a face and shouted, *"Baby!"* and then stomped off. I don't get what her problem is – after all, if she doesn't like me, why doesn't she just ignore me? Why does she have to trail round after me being horrible? I don't even know what she's got to be moody about – she's so lucky; her life's perfect and she's got *everything*. It's not like I even want to be friends with her, anyway. Not when she's mean, and lazy about looking after Gracie. It's like she doesn't even care about her own pony.

Oh, hang on, I can hear something. It sounds like crying. Let me just go and see…

11.24p.m. - well, I still can't sleep!

It was Arabella I could hear, crying in the bunk above me. I tried to ignore it, but she sounded so upset I couldn't. I climbed up the ladder and shone my torch on her. Her face was buried into the pillow and she was sobbing her heart out.

"What's wrong?" I whispered. "Are you feeling sick? Shall I get Jody?"

Arabella tried to speak but no words came out, just this coughing choking sound. "No, it's not that," she finally managed to mumble.

I pulled myself up and sat at the end of her bunk. To be honest, I felt really scared and I didn't know what to do. I was about to get Jody, when Arabella started talking. In a whisper she said, "No one likes me."

I thought about fibbing and saying *of course they do*, but I didn't feel like it. Instead I told her the truth. "That's because you're so mean to me."

"Only as a joke," she said weakly.

"Well, *ha ha*," I whispered. "It's pretty mean for a joke, you know. I don't understand you, Arabella. You've got everything. You're so—"

"I know you think I'm lucky, but I'm not," she muttered, then burst into fresh sobs.

 "Of course you are," I said. "You've got Gracie." I still felt pretty fed up with her. After all, I'd do anything to have my own pony!

"Gracie hates me," she snivelled.

"What?!" I cried, then clamped my hand over my mouth – I didn't want Jody to hear and come in to tell us off. "Is that what you think?" I asked, a lot more quietly. "Is that why you don't bother doing things for her?"

She nodded. "I know she doesn't want me near her so I try to stay away."

"But how can you think that?" I asked.

"Gracie's so sweet. She's a bit highly strung, maybe, but that's just her being an Arab mare. She's got a heart of gold."

Arabella sighed. "I've only had her for a few months, and we just don't seem to get along," she said then. "At the school stables she tried to kick me once when I was plaiting her tail. And she threw me off on a hack. And she keeps nipping me when I'm trying to tack her up." Tears ran down her face. "Sometimes I feel scared to be alone with her," she admitted.

That really shocked me. I could never be scared of Lucky, or think he hated me. We're such a team I just can't imagine it. "Maybe you should talk to Sally about it in the morning, she might have some ideas that will help," I suggested. Arabella still looked really upset so, even though I didn't want to, I added, "I'll come with you if you like."

She wiped her eyes. "Would you really?"

she asked. "Even after I've been so horrible to you?"

"Yeah, I suppose so," I muttered. "And, hey, what's that all about anyway? I've never done anything to you." I was trying to make it sound like no big deal, but actually I felt sick and my heart was pounding. Of course I've had fall outs with my friends and brothers, but no one's ever not liked me before, just over nothing.

Arabella was quiet for a long time. Then she finally said, "I guess I was jealous, because you're so lucky."

"Lucky!" I screeched, and I had to clamp my hand over my mouth again.

"Me?" I whispered.
"But you've got
everything! Freedom,
fun and Gracie.
How can you say
I'm lucky?"

"Your pony adores you, your family's there for you," she said simply. "I hardly ever see my mum and dad. They're not even coming to watch me ride on Friday. And being a boarder sounds fun, but it isn't that great in real life, well, not at my school anyway. The girls are always gossiping about each other and you have to get people on your side or you end up alone."

"Is that why you really wanted us two to be friends from the start?" I asked. "Because you thought you'd better get someone on your side?"

She nodded. "Yeah. But now I know it's different here. Like you said, there *are* no sides. Well, at least, there weren't until I messed everything up. Now no one likes me, and it's just me on my own against everybody else."

"It's not that bad," I began, but I trailed off because, basically, she was absolutely right.

"I'm so sorry, Lauren," she said then. "I'm really ashamed of how I've acted towards you.

I'm not surprised the others don't like me, either. But I'm going to change, I really am. Starting right now. I promise I'll make things up to you."

I didn't say anything. I didn't feel like making up with her. And besides, how could I trust she wouldn't start being mean to me again, as soon as we were in front of the others? "Oh, please, Lauren, give me another chance," she begged, bursting into tears again.

What could I say? She was really upset, and I did feel a little bit sorry for her after everything she'd told me. So in the end I agreed – we'd forget everything that's happened and make a fresh start, but only if she says sorry to Lucky, too!

When I was back down here in my own bunk, staring at nothing and thinking, I started to see that Arabella isn't so lucky after all. Yes, sleepovers at boarding school would be fun, but imagine having one every night and never being able to go home? Sure, having girls around all the time sounds great. But imagine having to worry all the time about who liked you and who didn't — it's not something I ever think about! And yes, my family is annoying sometimes, but they're all coming to see me on Friday, even Dad and Nana. Imagine having parents who'll buy you a pony, but are too busy to bother coming to see you ride it! And worst of all, imagine thinking your pony hates you!

Isn't it strange? Sometimes things aren't what they seem at all. And neither are people. Thinking about Arabella's life really makes me appreciate my own. She's right – I *am* the lucky one. I can't wait to give my gorgeous pony a big hug in the morning and tell him how lucky I feel to have him, too!

Actually, now I've written all this down I'm feeling a bit tired out myself. I'll just shut my eyes for a minute and

Thursday morning, during our break

I woke Arabella up early and Jody let us go down and speak to Sally before breakfast. She said she wouldn't allow it usually, but she could tell from our faces that it was important.

We went into the office and Sally was by the sink, filling the kettle. "Hi, girls," she said, "and what can I do for you this early? I haven't even had my coffee yet!"

I looked at Arabella and Arabella looked at the floor, and Sally looked at both of us and said, "Well?" So eventually I had to say, "Arabella's scared of Gracie, and we thought you might know what to do."

Sally looked confused.

"She hates me," Arabella said quietly.

69

"Oh, I'm sure that can't be true," said Sally, smiling. She was probably thinking it was just Arabella being difficult again.

"But she does," Arabella insisted. She glanced at me and I gave her a nod of encouragement. She took a deep breath and told Sally everything about Gracie nipping and kicking and throwing her off.

As Sally listened, her smile turned to a frown. "Well, I haven't noticed anything," she said.

"She doesn't do it when anyone else is around," said Arabella. "Only when I'm in the barn with her, when everyone's busy and distracted. She doesn't want anyone else to see what she's really like."

Sally sighed. "Ponies don't think like that," she said firmly. "It sounds as though you've got into a vicious circle. You're nervous when handling her, she picks up on it and gets anxious herself, then she acts up a bit and you get more nervous.

You need to break the cycle. You need to be calm and confident and in control."

"But she—" Arabella began, but Sally interrupted her.

"She doesn't *hate* you," she insisted. "As I said, ponies don't have those kind of thoughts."

"Really?" said Arabella.

"I promise," said Sally. "As someone who's had ponies since I was six, spent three years at equestrian college and five years as an instructor, I think I should know. But you do need to work on building up your relationship. Lauren's got a great partnership going with Lucky, I'm sure she can show you how it's done." She looked at me. "OK?"

I nodded.

"Thanks, Lauren," Arabella said shyly.

Sally smiled again then, and said, "Now, why don't you girls get yourselves in for some breakfast, before Millie scoffs all the

Frosted Wheats. And don't even think of coming down here this early again!"

"OK," said Arabella. She already looked much happier.

She went out into the yard and just as I was following, Sally called me back. "It's very kind of you to help her out," she said. "I've noticed that you two don't exactly get along."

I couldn't help smiling. "Maybe we will now," I said, and headed out.

So after breakfast, we all grabbed some lead ropes and went to catch our ponies. Lydia supervised us in the field, but she wouldn't do the catching for anyone this time. She said we should have the hang of it by now. After I'd caught Lucky, I noticed that Arabella was still standing in the field with her lead rope, looking uncertain. Tears sprang into her eyes and she said, "I tried, but whenever I start walking towards her, she just trots away."

"OK, don't worry," I told her. "Take a deep breath and think positive. Now walk up confidently to her side and clip on the lead rope, as if you *expect* her to stand still."

Arabella still looked unsure, but she did what I said. And guess what? It worked! She looked so pleased with herself, and she thanked me as we led our ponies out of the field. "See? She's a good girl," I said then. "She just needs to feel that you're confident and in control, that's all."

Gracie was a total sweetie on the yard, too.
I made sure I said loads of nice things about her
so that Arabella could see how lovely she is.
I showed her how to run her hand down
Gracie's side and leg before trying to pick up
her hooves, so that she didn't get a shock. Then
when she was trying to sponge her eyes Gracie
did a loud snort and tossed her head. Arabella
started and jumped backwards, but I just
grinned and said, "Don't worry, she's only saying
thank you!" Arabella saw it
differently then and gave
Gracie a big pat, so
we're definitely getting
somewhere already!

Oh, and guess what?
Arabella *did* say sorry to Lucky, too! And she
made a big fuss of him, patting his neck and
telling him what a clever boy he was and how
fab he is going to be in the dressage comp.

He whinnied and nuzzled her arm, so I know he forgave her – and I'm sure the half a carrot she gave him must have helped, too!

Arabella was also a bit nervous of the other dressagers after what happened yesterday evening, but she took a deep breath and put on a big smile. And it worked 'cos soon everyone was happily grooming away in the yard. Then when she was about to start using the mane comb on Gracie's body Paula pointed to it and went, "Beep! Uh-uh!" as if we were still playing quizzes. Everyone laughed and it was so funny that Arabella couldn't help joining in. I grinned at her and she grinned back. Perhaps she's not so bad after all.

Oh, hang on, here come the others.

In bed – I'm tired out but too excited to sleep, so I'll just catch up on my diary

We had our lesson first this morning, so we could practise riding our freestyle tests to our music. Then during the workshop time Sally gave us notes on how we did. We were all nervous and excited about putting everything together at last. Lydia called out the dressage tests for us, so we could focus on our riding. We'll have to have them memorized and go it alone tomorrow, though!

After a warm-up on each rein and some general work on balance and impulsion, it was time to ride the tests. The rest of us went out into the lane to give each rider the whole manège. We dismounted, held on to our ponies, and while they munched on the grass verge, we leaned on the fence to watch.

Gracie started getting a bit restless and Arabella gave me an anxious glance. She was gripping tightly on to the lead rope, so no wonder the poor pony was getting fed up. I told her to relax, let the rope out and give Gracie a bit of space. She did, and soon Gracie was happily munching on the grass verge.

"Thanks!" said Arabella. Then she burst out laughing. "*And* for the lovely gungy green bit I'm going to have to scrub!"

I couldn't help laughing too, especially when I saw that Lucky had a foaming green mouth to match Gracie's! Urgh!

I was third up after Paula and Marie. I really enjoyed myself – it felt completely different doing the test to music. Lucky was more alert and quicker off the leg, so I knew he definitely liked the song I'd chosen! Thank goodness Lydia was calling out the test though, because I would have forgotten all about our halt and rein back at E and gone walking all the way up the long side! I just hope I can get it firmly into my head before tomorrow.

I was really into the rhythm of the music and I focused on using squeezes on and half halts to get Lucky exactly on the beat. This didn't always work and it's really tricky to do, but when it did it looked great, so even if I can just get *some* of my routine like that tomorrow I'll be happy!

After Leonie and Arabella had had their goes we all went back into the manège and warmed down together, and then took our ponies back to the barn and untacked. We were all saying well done to each other and keeping our fingers crossed for good comments from Sally.

fingers crossed!

Once we'd grabbed drinks and sat down at the benches, Sally gave us her notes. Everyone has points to work on, but me and Lucky seem to have a LOT! They are:

1. Make sure I know the test off by heart without it being called.

2. Use the trot down the centre line when we first come in to get Lucky listening and awake, by using half halts and squeezing on.

3. Don't worry too much about the lengthened trot strides through X – just normal trot strides are fine. (Phew, 'cos we were having lots of trouble getting those right!)

4. Keep my head up and look where I'm going – not down Lucky's neck!

5. Keep on the track during my canters – don't allow Lucky to cut the corners off.

When Sally had given us all our notes, she said, "So, let's recap. What does the judge expect to see?" We could just reel off the answer by now because she'd said it so many times, and we all chanted: "Rhythm, impulsion, suppleness, expression, on the bit, straight, good collection, good rider position," and then burst into fits of giggles.

"OK, well done," she said, rolling her eyes. Then she put us in pairs to carry on memorizing our tests, and when I went with Marie, Arabella didn't get moody about it, she just asked if we could be a three. Marie said yes and it worked out fine.

When we came out after lunch we were all stressing out about how much practice we still needed to do before the freestyle comp, and all the points we've got to improve on. But when we got on to the yard, Sally really surprised us by saying, "Actually, what you girls need far more than practice is to chill out! It's a beautiful afternoon and we're going for a hack!"

At first we were all going, "No, we can't! We really *do* need to practise!" But soon we were having a great time with our ponies, cantering up stubble fields and trotting down lanes – we even had to go through a river! At one point, Flame stumbled over a branch on the ground and Paula came tumbling off, and later on Arabella said to me that she could see Flame didn't do it on purpose and so maybe Gracie hadn't either when she'd pitched *her* off that time. She even admitted at tea that going on the hack was the best thing we could have done because she could bond with Gracie and have fun. (I was amazed because she's so obsessed with dressage practice usually.) In fact, when we were grooming down and caring for our ponies it was *me* going, "Come on, hurry up, I'm hungry," because Arabella didn't want to leave Gracie!

Then this evening the fun continued 'cos we had...

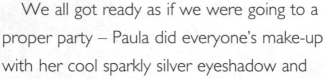

A last night disco!

We all got ready as if we were going to a proper party – Paula did everyone's make-up with her cool sparkly silver eyeshadow and

pink lipgloss, and
Bea lent me her silky
red flower clip 'cos
she was wearing her
blue one.

Jody drew the curtains and Millie's big brother James brought his light system into the games room (so I guess brothers are useful sometimes!). We all had a great time dancing about, and after a few songs James would just suddenly mix in one of our dressage test tunes. When that happened we would all stand back and let the girl whose song it was pretend to be on her pony and mark out the test. It was so funny, my jaw was aching from laughing so much, especially at Leonie 'cos when her *Black Beauty* music came on she kept whinnying and pretending her pony was messing about!

Neigh-hey-hey-hey!

I can't wait for the comp tomorrow. I don't think me and Lucky are going to be exactly brilliant, especially not against Paula and Flame, but we're going to try our best and have lots of fun while we're at it!

Friday – it's the big day and I'm so excited about the comp!

We're all ready and we're just waiting for the parents to arrive. I'm really looking forward to seeing my bunch again – I've missed them loads (OK, I admit it, even my stinky bros!).

This morning we had our final lesson (boo hoo!). We went over the compulsory movements together as a ride, and then we each tried out our tests to music. I was amazed at how much has sunk in simply by us messing round at the disco yesterday, and I have definitely fixed points 1, 4 and 5 on my list! We had one go each and then Sally said, "That's it, enough, I don't want you to be over-rehearsed." (Like, as if *that* could happen!) Then we got ourselves and our ponies ready, and cleaned our tack until it shone.

Now we look like this:

Arabella & Gracie

Leonie & Charm

Paula & Flame

me & Lucky

Marie & Mischief

Oh, hey, that's my parents' car!

I'm writing this at home in my own bed – I can't believe Pony Camp is over!

I'm going to carry on exactly where I stopped writing so that I don't leave out anything important!

So, all the parents arrived – well, all except Arabella's. I felt really sad for her when everyone was kissing and hugging each other, so I pulled her over to my mum and Nana and they gave her a big hug too, then all my brothers joined in and she nearly got squished (their hugs are more like being hit by dodgems)!

It really seemed to cheer her up and I realized again that I am really, really lucky to have my lot, even if it can get loud and boyish in our house sometimes!

We watched Group A do their gymkhana games and we all cheered really loudly for them. Millie was amazing and would have won everything, of course, if she hadn't accidentally-on-purpose let Tally gallop off the wrong way in some of the races! Bea and Jojo both won a race and Polly won two, so they were all really pleased with themselves.

Then it was time for our group to go and get our ponies and mount up for the freestyle dressage – EEEEEEEEEEEEEEK!

I offered for me and Lucky to go last, because no one else fancied it, and also because Lucky is the most chilled of all the ponies and he was happy to wait, even with all the noise and kerfuffle going on.

CHILLED PONY

The crowd absolutely loved the dressage and went crazy clapping after each person's turn. Everyone laughed when Marie's "Uh Oh, We're In Trouble" song came on, because it suited

Mischief perfectly! They rode a great test, too, although cheeky Mischief trotted on after the mark where he should have come back to walk a couple of times and did an extra 20 metre circle in canter, just because he was enjoying himself so much!

Paula's Spanish flamenco-themed test was especially amazing – really dramatic with lots of sudden halts and changes of pace, including (can you believe!) halt to *canter*.

Leonie was fantastic! Her entrance was brill – she launched straight into canter in perfect time with her *Black Beauty* music and everyone did a loud cheer! As she prepared for her counter-canter we all had our fingers crossed for her that it would go OK, and it did! She got it perfect and she looked just like the pros we'd seen at the county show!

When Arabella's music from the ballet of
Romeo and Juliet came bursting out of the
speakers, all the other girls and my family gave
her a massive cheer to encourage her. I think it
really spurred her on, because she did a great
test. They only had one problem, with getting a
canter in the AF corner, so they had to circle
round again, but she kept smiling and didn't get
stressed about it, so Gracie followed her lead
and didn't either.

As Arabella was doing her test, I started
feeling really excited, but nervous as well –
I didn't want to muck up my routine in front
of my whole family. I was getting a bit wound
up and then I remembered the advice that I
had given Arabella only yesterday, which was
to chill out, relax and have fun. So I took a
deep breath and forced myself to put on a big
smile, and soon I was grinning for real. When it
was me and Lucky's turn to go into the arena

I leaned down and gave him a big pat and whispered in his ear, "Let's give it our best shot!"

And, well, we definitely did that!

Everyone loved me twirling my umbrella on the way in and gave a big cheer, which made me feel really confident! (I passed it to Lydia before we started the test, of course.)

It was so brilliant going round to our music with my fab pony – just like we were dancing together. We didn't do enough steps of rein back, I forgot how many it was supposed to be, and I went on to the left rein again at A instead of changing and doing everything like a mirror on the right rein. But I corrected it quickly by doing a loop back in the AK corner and kept smiling, so I don't think anyone noticed – well, except Sally and Lydia, of course!

At the end we got to X and made a square halt (hooray!). Just as the song finished with the words "I'd do anything, anything for you", Lucky snorted and shook his head like he was agreeing and everyone went "Ahhh!" 'cos he looked so cute. I was so proud of him, of us, that I felt like I might burst. If it had been a comp for the most gorgeous pony we definitely would have won! We didn't, of course – Sally said it was a really close call between Paula and Leonie, but in the end she awarded Leonie first prize and Paula second. Something totally amazing did happen though – me and Lucky came third (and got a gorgeous green rosette)! There wasn't a fourth or fifth place, but Marie and Arabella got these lovely pink rosettes too, for taking part.

I thought Arabella might be a bit moody with me for coming ahead of her, but in fact she gave me a big hug and said well done (and made a fuss of Lucky, too).

When I said well done back to her, she just
shrugged. "Not really that well," she said. "We
couldn't get our canter, and I lost the rhythm of
the music a couple of times and—"

"But you worked together, and you both
looked comfortable and relaxed, and anyone
could tell Gracie was really listening to you,"
I pointed out. "Those things are much more
important than getting it technically perfect."

"Thanks," she said. "And thanks for all your
help with Gracie. We couldn't have done any of
it without you. You'd make a great instructor,
you know."

I couldn't help beaming when she said that.
I imagined myself in Sally's shoes in a few years'
time. I'd love that more than anything
 in the world. Well, maybe if I
work hard on my riding, and help
out a lot at my local stables, and
read up on pony care, who

knows, perhaps I'll be able to get into equestrian college, too!

Of course, my dad videoed everything, like he always does, and he said he'll burn a copy of it for Arabella so she can show her parents when she visits them next. She looked a bit upset when he mentioned them, but Mum gave her another hug and said she bet they were really wishing they could be here with us at Pony Camp, and how she was sure they were fed up with being stuck at work far away in another country.

I hadn't thought of it like that before, and perhaps Arabella hadn't either, because she seemed to cheer up even more then.

When it was time to go home I spent ages in the barn with Lucky, making sure he had enough water and checking his hooves for

stones and just giving him loads and loads of
hugs and telling him how much I love him.
Plus, I said I'll look at his picture every day and
never forget him, and try to persuade
Mum to let me come back next
year. He nuzzled into my shoulder
and snorted gently, so I know he
felt just like I did.

All the other girls were the same – none of
us wanted to leave our ponies. We were all
taking whole group pics and snaps of us with our
ponies, and Polly even asked me to take one of
her mucking out a poo to show her brother she
really did do it 'cos he didn't believe she would!

Finally it was really absolutely, definitely time
to go (in Sally's words) so we all had a few final
photos with her and Lydia and Jody and Millie,
and then we started heading off to our cars.

Arabella was staying till we'd all gone,
because Jody was driving her back to her

boarding school later on with Gracie in the horsebox, then she's off to the Lake District to do outdoor activities. She gave me another big hug and we kept saying goodbye and then starting to talk again, until Mum had to pretty much order me into the car! We're going to write to each other and Mum says perhaps she can come and stay at the end of the holidays. I can't believe we've ended up being such good friends after everything that's happened!

I'm just so lucky that I went to Pony Camp and that I got Lucky the pony, and I'm also so lucky to have such a caring family.

Oh, gotta go, Mum's calling me down to set the table for tea. Groan! I think I'll go and ask her why my bros can't help, and I'll keep how lucky I feel to myself!

Lauren 🍀

For Tom, with huge thanks for all your
wonderful work on Pony Camp xx

With special thanks to our cover stars,
Hannah and Mac, pony guru Janet Rising
and our fab photographer, Zoe Cannon.

www.kellymckain.co.uk

STRIPES PUBLISHING
An imprint of Magi Publications
1 The Coda Centre, 189 Munster Road, London SW6 6AW

A paperback original
First published in Great Britain in 2009

Text copyright © Kelly McKain, 2009
Illustrations copyright © Mandy Stanley, 2009
Cover photograph copyright © Zoe Cannon, 2009

ISBN: 978-1-84715-074-5

A CIP catalogue record for this book is available from the British Library.

Printed in Belgium

2 4 6 8 10 9 7 5 3 1